To matthew,
P's out on books!
Aaron Copland 1988

PRISCILLA

PRISCILLA

By COLENE COPELAND
Illustrated By EDITH HARRISON

JORDAN VALLEY HERITAGE HOUSE

PRISCILLA

Manufactured in the United States of America

Library of Congress Catalog
Card number: 81-80663

ISBN: 0-939810-01-8 (Hardcover)
ISBN: 0-939810-02-6 (Softcover)

Fifth Printing

To my loving husband Bob,
who willingly shared our home and our vacation
with a special little pig.

AUTHOR'S NOTE

Priscilla was a real live pig ----not a figment of my imagination. In fact, all of the animals named in this book were real.

Although Priscilla adds a little color now and then in the telling, the "events" in the story actually took place.

CONTENTS

Chapter 1.

TOO BIG FOR THE HOUSE

MAMA had always let me sit on her lap to watch television. How was I to know that one day she would say, "Priscilla! You are *too* heavy for me to hold." She picked me up and gently tucked me in, by her side, on the couch.

Mama looked uneasy. "The time has come to move you out to the barn," she said.

The barn? How could she suggest such a thing? What do I know about living in a barn? *Nothing!* That's what.

Papa looked amused, "Who's going to teach her to act like a pig?" he asked.

"My Priscilla is *very* bright. She'll learn," Mama answered. "I hate to see her grow up. She's the cleanest pet I've ever had in the house. Wish there was some shot we could give her to keep her from getting any bigger."

1

"But there isn't," Papa said. He picked me up and put me on his lap. "She knows people, Mama. But this kindhearted little thing wouldn't last ten minutes with a batch of hogs. She's strong enough now, but she's pure pet."

"That's right, dear. We must be careful how we handle her transition from the house to the barn," Mama said. "I wouldn't have her hurt for the world."

Papa's question bothered me. "Who is going to teach her to act like a pig?" he had said. I wonder what he meant by that. It's not my fault if I don't act like a pig. If anyone is to blame it should be an old sow named Mabel, my real mother. *Some mother* she is! Doesn't even like me. My own mother! She laid all five hundred pounds of herself on me the day I was two days old! Lucky for me Papa and Mama were near and heard me squealing. They got there just in time. Papa poked Mabel real hard, trying to get her up off of me. She finally raised one shoulder. Mama lifted me out, thinking I was dead. I *nearly* was.

They took me to the house. I don't remember the first few days, but I know Mama took care of me. I drank milk from a baby's bottle and slept on the bed with my new parents. Mama's poodle, Mitzi, "housebroke" me. I noticed she scratched on the back door when she wanted out. So, I did it too. I even went to California in the car with Mama and Papa, on vacation. I'll tell you more about that later.

When I was feeling better, Mama tried to give me back to my mother, but she wouldn't take me back. She pushed me away. Mabel didn't want to be bothered with me. Makes me sad to think about it. Sometimes, it makes me mad!

Papa's eyes were closed and his head was tilted back against his chair. I think he was worried about me too. "Mama, do you think Priscilla understands what we're saying?"

"Of course. Every word," she answered.

"You're awfully sure of yourself," Papa chuckled.

"I *am* sure," Mama told him. "Remember the day we brought her in from Mabel's pen?"

"I remember," he answered drowsily.

"Right away, I named her 'Priscilla'. The name fits her perfectly. I told her we love her and would not let her die. She understood. She *still* understands. -----every word." Mama was positive.

"If you say so, Mama," Papa said. He was not convinced.

All I could think about was getting moved out. I would be put in a pig pen, no doubt. What will it be like? Papa said I wouldn't last ten minutes with a batch of hogs. Maybe I'll be *killed* right away! Golly! I don't want to think about it.

But Mama said she wouldn't have me hurt for the world. So, I guess I'll just have to wait and see.

Sometimes, when Papa and Mama go out to feed the hogs and clean the pens, my friend Mitzi and I go along. I like that. We run around in the back of the station wagon. Once in a while Mitzi gets to bark at dogs in other cars, but I never, ever, see another pig in a car.

When our Oregon weather is agreeable Mitzi and I play outside. We race around the barns. She sniffs and smells everything. I root up the ground. I don't know why I root up the ground. It just seems like the thing to do.

We love to pester the nanny goats. They get mad and stomp their feet and give us dirty looks.

The chickens outsmart us. When they see us coming they fly up in the trees. That really aggravates Mitzi. She doesn't like to be outdone by a chicken.

One day I peeked inside the farrowing barn, the place where big sows go when they are about ready to have their babies, or whenever they are looking for a husband. What a racket! There were noisy, ill-mannered sounds of eating. Someone was *slurping* water.

Papa had been hauling cedar shavings in the old red wheelbarrow. Just as I was about to go in, so was he.

"Come on in, Priscilla," he invited. "Look the place over. You will be spending time in this barn, someday."

I stood in the wide doorway. I could hear little pigs' voices, but I couldn't see them.

There was one big sow in each of the pens. Some of them stared at me. One yelled!

"Hey, pig! Why aren't you in the feeder building?" she croaked, in an unladylike voice. I was too frightened to answer.

"You there, pig," she shouted, "I'm *talking* to you. Can't you hear?" No one had ever spoken to me so cruelly before.

Finally, I mustered up enough nerve to say, "I don't live in the feeder barn. I live in the house with Mama and Papa." I turned my eyes away from her cold unfriendly stare and looked for Papa.

"What! —You live where, with who?" she mocked.

"I live in the house with Mama and Papa," I repeated shyly.

She began to laugh fiendishly. The others joined her. They all turned their attention to me and shouted loud, cold-hearted remarks. Someone called me "Little Miss Super Pet". Another one said, "The dumb little creep doesn't know she's a pig."

I couldn't see anything funny to laugh about. I began to cry.

Mitzi heard the commotion. She saw my predicament. "Don't pay any attention to those ugly old hogs, Priscilla. They are *jealous* of you. Come on," she coaxed. "Let's go for a run in the orchard."

"You go ahead," I blubbered. Tears were streaming down my face. I hurried around to the side of the barn, out of sight. I could still hear them laughing. I felt terrible.

Never, will I forget *that* day. How can I make Mama and Papa understand? Hogs don't like me!

Chapter 2.

A NEW HOME FOR ME

THAT night I slept a restless sleep. I dreamed terrible, frightening dreams! Seven monstrous black sows attacked me! They snapped me up with their tough snouts and tossed me about like a Kansas cyclone! I wiggled and jerked and managed to escape! But as soon as I was free from them an army of scarlet, long tusked boars, charged me from every direction! They were blood thirsty! There was no escape! I was doomed to suffer their torture! They pinched, bit, slapped and shook me! They knocked me down, kicked me and spit on me! All the while they laughed a gory laugh. I suffered great pain! They seemed to relish my agony.

Mama was in my dream. I could hear her voice but I could not see her. "Pris---cil---la," she called to me.

My enemies continued to tear at my flesh!

Mama's voice grew nearer. Finally, I saw her running toward me. A thick grey mist boiled up all around her. She could not reach me.

Suddenly, a great white sow came charging through the mist! Her unexpected presence startled my abductors! She rushed toward me gently lifting me on her strong nose. She tossed me to Mama. I knew I was safe----at last.

What a nightmare! I tried to wake up. I was crying so hard my head ached. My heart was pounding so fast I bounced off my pillow. I tumbled to and fro. My head banged against the bedroom wall. *That* woke me up.

My pillow was wet with tears.

Slowly, I stood up on rubbery legs and checked my body for scars. How lucky for me to survive such an ordeal. I thought of the beautiful white sow who had saved me from utter destruction.

I chose to stay awake for the rest of the night. Going back to bed could mean having another of those *awful* dreams. I certainly couldn't risk having *that* happen!

Slipping quietly out of the bedroom I headed for the living room. I flipped on the television with my nose and jumped up on the sofa. A young man in a red checked shirt was giving the early morning farm report. I was in no mood to hear about the price of hogs. So, I crawled in under an oversized sofa pillow until some music came on.

Before long the little gold alarm clock by the bed began to ring. Quickly, I turned off the T.V., dashed to the bedroom and jumped on my pillow. No need to worry Mama and Papa about my restless night. I did not want to be troublesome.

Mitzi bounced around on the bed, waking up Mama and Papa. She looked silly. Mitzi sleeps between the pillows on the bed. I *used* to sleep there, when I was smaller. Lately, my bed has been a big soft pillow on the floor, on Mama's side of the bed.

Frequently, in the night, when I get scared or lonesome, I hop up on the bed and snuggle up between Papa and Mama. Papa grumbles about it, but Mama just scratches my ears and says, "Go back to sleep, Priscilla." So I do.

Mitzi ran straight for the kitchen door, barking. Papa let us out. We darted to the back yard.

Even though the grass was wet, this was my favorite time to be in the back yard. The skinny lady next door would still be sleeping. She often peeks over the fence at us and gives us dirty looks.

Mitzi and I checked out the entire back yard to see if any dogs had paid us a visit during the night. None had. A spotted frog hopped along under the lilac bush. An Oregon bluejay sat on a fence post and squawked. He thinks he owns the back yard. But Mitzi and I know better.

A couple of walnuts were lying on the ground. Just as I was about to sink my teeth into one, Mama called, "Breakfast is ready!" *Scrud!* I *wanted* those nuts!

We raced to the house! Mitzi let me win today. Mama held the door open and laughed when I wiped my feet on the mat.

"You are the cleanest pet I've ever had in the house, Priscilla," she said with a smile in her voice. I've heard her say that before. It must be a fact.

"I'll bet we're the only people in the world who own a pig who lives in the house and wipes its feet on the mat to boot," Papa chuckled.

I like it when they say nice things about me. Mitzi would get bragged on too if she would wipe her feet on the mat. But she just stands there until Mama wipes the morning dew from her feet, with a rag.

Breakfast was delicious. I had a bottle of warm milk, plus--- Mitzi's leftovers.

I listened to every word that was said at breakfast. I sort of hung around under the table. Crumbs drop on the floor sometimes. But with me around they never know it.

"Priscilla has to be with her own kind," Mama said. "I hate to put her out! Is there no other way, dear?"

"We have no right to keep her from a normal life! Someday she will want pigs of her own. Right now --- she's so tame! It will be easier if she can make the adjustment now while she's young," he answered.

Babies of my *own?* Gee! I had never thought about being a ----mother!

Doomsday arrived! I was whisked away to the station wagon. Mama was crying. I felt awful. Nobody said a word while Papa drove the three miles to the hog barns. I didn't feel like looking out the windows or running around in the back. I settled for a spot on the front seat and kept quiet.

The road became bumpy. Gravel peppered the bottom of the car. I knew without looking we had arrived at the farm.

The hogs shouted the news of our coming to each other. Papa's arrival meant breakfast would soon be served. I'll bet they wouldn't be so anxious if they knew that I was moving in!

Curiosity overtook me. I gathered my courage and took a peek out the window. Papa drove past the farrowing barn. Boy! What a relief! He breezed by two more buildings and then another. *Where* are they taking me?

We moved on, through the old orchard. Two nanny goats stood still and followed us with their eyes. We passed the empty sheep shed. Papa doesn't like sheep all that much.

Finally! We came to a stop by the lofty, newly restored machine shed. The old roof had been replaced. Walls that were once windowless boasted shiny clean panes.

Mitzi and I had checked this building out plenty of times. Except for Papa's tractor, it's empty.

There was a fenced yard in the front of the shed, a nice addition! The fence was put together in sections of unpainted wood. Each section was attached to small square posts which had been set in the ground. A bright green gate led us into the yard.

Papa directed us to a sliding door cut in the front of the shed. He gave it a saucy little shove to the right. The door flew open. And, *there it was!* A brand new pen. Entirely unused. Wasn't hard to guess who it was built for!

The pen was much larger than those in the farrowing barn. Yet, it sort of got lost in such an overgrown building. The little pen looked ----lonely.

I had no idea it would be so *private* and ----safe.

"Look it over, Priscilla," Mama said. "It's all yours."

So *this* is where I'll be living, not with other hogs,

but *here*, by myself, away from everybody. How strange! Hadn't Mama said I should be with my own kind? Am I the *only one* of my kind? Are there no others like me? Am I to be *alone, forever?* How could they do this to me?

I looked at my "parents" and fought back the tears. I would *not* cry. I did not want to be troublesome. After all, hadn't they built this pen especially for me. It *was* nice, *really* nice.

The floor was made of smooth wood and covered with fresh, sweet smelling cedar shavings. Once, I saw a dance floor on television, just like this. The floor looked inviting. I ran a few feet and put on my brakes. Wow! Did I go sliding. I did it again and again. Shavings flew every which way! It was fun. I was having a good time.

Suddenly, I spied the inviting pile of golden wheat straw that lay in one corner. I jumped right in, crawled underneath and ran out the other side with pieces of straw on my head. Mitzi would love this place, I thought.

Papa and Mama laughed at my buffoonery. They like seeing me happy.

"I think she likes this place," Papa said. "Let's leave her be for now. We're late with the chores."

I could see it pained Mama to leave me. She kept looking back as they left the building.

Maybe it won't be so bad here, I thought.

As soon as I was alone I began to snoop. First I checked out my yard. There was a sunken grassy spot. I didn't like it until I discovered how well my body fit into it, a perfect spot for sun bathing.

There was a new metal oil drip pan filled with fresh drinking water. It won't be the same as home! At home, Mitzi had a water dish. When no one was looking, I'd take a sip. Water always tasted better to me from a baby's bottle. It had its benefits. I got more attention with the bottle, also back rubs and conversation. *Now*, when I'm thirsty, I'll have to drink from this old pan.

There were two doors on my pen, the sliding door that leads to the yard and a swinging gate that opens up to the inside of the machine shed. Inside, by the gate, sat a wooden "V" shaped box. There was nothing in it. Perhaps it's a waste paper basket. I'll have to ask Mama.

The pen was nice and neat when we arrived. But not now! I had really messed up the place. The floor, once evenly covered with cedar shavings, had ugly looking bare streaks where I had slid. My straw was scattered like confetti after a New Year's eve party. I saw that on television too, in a late late movie. Suspecting the straw was my bed, common sense told me if I wanted a nice place to sleep I'd better clean house. And, I wanted Mama to be proud of me.

I rooted around in the shavings until the floor

looked presentable. With a little fluffing up, the straw proved to be quite comfortable. It was different than my pillow behind the bed, much different. But then, those comforts are gone ----gone forever.

As I lay there in wonderment, I had a most peculiar feeling, a very strange sensation, as if I were being watched. No one was in sight. I could see the nannies in the orchard and a few chickens pecked around the exposed roots of a knobby tree, but *they* weren't looking my way.

Who would want to look at me? No one will ever care for me except Mama and Papa. I'll be lonesome here.

Mama returned carrying a bucket. She poured something that looked like cereal in the "V" shaped box.

"Come on, Priscilla," she said. "I want you to try some of these pig pellets. They're made of corn and alfalfa and lots of other good stuff to help you grow. The other pigs eat them and like them a lot. Come and try some."

Well now! Let's see what pigs eat. I got up and looked at it. It smelled like bread, but it was crunchy little pieces. I tried a couple. They were o.k. but I wasn't hungry. Besides. there was that feeling again that someone was watching me, and it wasn't Mama.

I felt silly as I glanced about. I was scared! Maybe I should tell Mama! Maybe not. I'd be embarrassed.

"You're going to be o.k., Priscilla," Mama assured me. "I'll be back after a bit." She patted me on the head and noticed how clean my place was. "No one would *ever* believe how you've straightened this place up. You are something else, Priscilla!" She left.

"But Mama," I said, after she had gone, "I'll be lonesome here." I began to cry.

Chapter 3.

T.C.

I cocked my head and strained to follow the sound of the station wagon as it rumbled softly away on the bumpy gravel road. Then for a long while, I pondered my situation. One of a kind! That's me! I fall far short of being *in the know* when it comes to *pig know how,* can *scarcely* be called a *person,* knowing full well I act like one. Yet, here I am, isolated from pigs and people and the whole wide world. I'm all alone, and yet, there is that constant feeling of being watched! Maybe it's God! Hadn't Mama said that God would watch over me?

Suddenly, a husky voice burst forth from the sky "Been moved out, huh?"

"Wha----?" I whirled around! Cedar shavings flew every which way! *Seeing* nothing, I dived into my straw pile and hid! Only my tail stuck out. I was so frightened my body shook all over, causing the entire

18

straw stack to quiver!

The voice laughed. It *sounded* friendly.

Slowly, I stuck my head out to have a look. But I still didn't see anyone.

I came right to the point. "Are you God?"

The voice laughed again. "Mercy no! But I do know a lot of females who sort of glorify me. Some think me to be quite princely. Sort of a Prince Charming, maybe. But, sacred, Lordly? -----I kinda doubt it."

"Where are you please?" I asked politely thinking it might be God ----teasing me.

"Up here. In the tractor seat," it said.

I looked up. There he sat, in Papa's big tractor seat, grinning down at me.

"You're not God! You're a cat!" I said, a little disappointed.

"Oh! I've always known that. *You* are the one who thought I was God," he answered as he raised up and flexed his muscles. "I kinda liked it, you thinking I was God. It had a nice ring to it."

It was plain to see this cat lacked humility! He *really* liked himself a lot. But he *was* friendly and it would be wonderful to have a friend.

"You really *scared* me, cat!" I scolded. "I don't think it's nice to spy on people! You *have* been watching me. Haven't you?"

"Sure have," he answered shamelessly. "There's

not much excitement around here. A guy can get pretty bored, even a little lonesome."

"You? Lonesome?" I asked, *very* surprised. How could a character like this tom cat ever find time to be lonesome? Perhaps he was just trying to make me feel good.

"Sure! I'm normal you know. Well ----almost, anyway," he laughed. "Lately I've been watching 'em put up this new home of yours. Pretty fancy pad for a porker! Do you know you're the only pig on the place with private living quarters? Not to mention your own fenced yard."

"Honest? I am?"

"Betcha didn't know you were *that* special," he said as he began his descent from the tractor seat landing on the top boards of my pen. How graceful he is! As well as being the most handsome he was by far the largest cat I had ever seen. Of course, I haven't seen very many.

His coat was short but not harsh. There were black pencilled markings to the head, forming an "M" on the face. More swirls were on his cheeks, rings around the eyes and chest and more dark swirls and stripes here and there over the rest of him. I could see greys and white underneath a lot of black tips. He looked a lot like Tiger, the tabby who lives in the house, except for size. He was well proportioned, for a cat. But I dare not tell him for fear he would become more vain than ever.

His majesty settled himself on a corner post of my pen and peered down upon me through large round eyes.

To think, I had actually mistaken this cat, for God! The best I could hope for was that God was busy with someone else and had not noticed how I had made a fool of myself.

If God was listening to either of us it was probably the cat. Why? Because the cat liked being called God. He said it had a nice ring to it.

But there he sat, smiling. What do you say to a guy like this?

"Do you know all the other pigs?" I asked.

"Certainly," he answered.

"I've never been around any other pigs. I've lived in the house with Mama and Papa since I was just two days old," I said.

"I know all that," the cat told me. "By the way, they call me T.C. ---That's short for Tom Cat."

"Pleased to meet you," I said. "I am called Priscilla. Priscilla isn't short for anything, but Mama told me once that my name comes from the Roman word, Priscus. Priscus means *former*."

"Oh! That's nice," he said. "-------I think." We both laughed a little. I was having a real good time.

"I was ---wondering. Do you think we can be friends?" I asked shyly.

"Sure kid! Why not? A guy can't have too many friends. When I saw you down here in your pen all alone and feeling sorry for yourself, I said to myself, 'Self, be a good scout and go down there. Be a friend to that lonely little porker.' So, knowing good and well that I give good advice, I took it." The Tom Cat was playing my big brother. I liked it.

He continued. "We've all known for a long time that the Mr. and Mrs. wouldn't keep you away from your own kind much longer. In fact, I've been taking all bets that you would be here today."

"You have? The Mr. and Mrs.? Is that what you call Mama and Papa?" I asked eagerly.

"Everybody but you, Priscilla," he laughed.

"So what? They will always be Mama and Papa to me. And, you shouldn't bet. It isn't nice," I scolded.

"It is when you've got a cinch bet. My brother, Tiger. He gave me the exact date."

"Tiger, is your brother?" I was surprised!

"Yep, but we have different fathers," he grinned. His remark made me blush.

That conniving scoundrel. How clever he is. With the exact date of my arrival from Tiger, he did have a cinch bet!

Although T.C. was the only friend I had around at the present, I didn't want him to think *he* was the only friend I had. I told him that Tiger was a friend of mine, also Mitzi and Cleo. The fact that Cleo was only a baby chicken was information I did not care to share. For now, at least, I chose not to mention it.

"By the way, Tom Cat, how come I haven't seen you around here before?" I asked.

"Well I've seen *you* enough times running in and out of buildings and rooting up grass in the orchard. Problem is, you're always with that dog. Me and the mutts don't hit it off. Never did. When I spy one in my domain I climb a tree and hope it gets bitten by a billy goat. ---Barking bugs me." T.C. was serious.

I was shocked to hear that Mitzi was his enemy. She is my best friend. Tiger and Mitzi get along fine. It was hard for me to understand T.C.'s feelings. In the house everybody got along together. Lots of times Mitzi, Tiger, Cleo and I all crawled into the same box in the house and took naps, because we ----- loved each other.

"Do other cats like you?" I asked.

"That's a *dumb* question. *Of course* other cats like me. Why shouldn't they?" He was disturbed by the idea that anyone would dislike him.

"I don't think the other pigs will like me!" I said, revealing my greatest fear and feeling once again like crying.

T.C. quickly assured me that other pigs *will* like me. But I was not so sure. I could not forget the day I followed Papa into the farrowing barn and how those big sows made fun of me. I thought of my dream and the hogs who tried to kill me.

When bed time came I missed Mama and Papa and Mitzi. I missed my bottle of warm milk. It was hard to be brave but I knew I must try to act like a pig, although I wasn't too sure how a pig acts. I did not want to be troublesome.

T.C. was over in a far corner of the machine shed eating a mouse. It looked terrible! What a mess! How could *anybody* eat a mouse?

I mosied over and tried to eat some pellets, but I had no appetite. If I couldn't eat maybe I could sleep. I fluffed up my straw and lay down. I couldn't sleep either. I wanted to go home. Why did I have to get too big for the house? Would I ever see another pig? I was *so* lonely.

Chapter 4.

GETTING A SECRET TREAT

A car pulled up. It was Mama and Papa and Mitzi. T.C. leaped up to the rafters and looked down. I was anxious to tell them about my new friend.

"You're not eating your food, Priscilla!" Papa sounded aggravated. I'll have to try harder, I thought, not wanting to be troublesome. I dashed right over to my feed box and gulped down a few pellets.

"We'll just have to wait and see," Mama said.

"Wait and see for what?" Papa asked.

"To see if she *will* eat and adjust to this pig pen." Mama answered. She sank down on my straw. I ran over and jumped in her lap and very quickly got shoved off.

"Priscilla," she yelled, "you can't do that anymore. You're just too darned heavy."

She scared me! I plunged for the far side of the

26

pen. Mama was laughing.

"I didn't mean to scare you, Darling," she said playfully. "Come here --lie beside me --put your head in my lap."

I accepted the invitation. Turned out to be o.k. for me. Mama rubbed my back and said, "God loves you, my Priscilla. He will watch over you when Papa and I aren't around."

There she was again, talking about God. I told her about T.C. She thought it was pretty funny that I should mistake him for God.

Papa had raced off to check a sow who was due to have babies soon. When he was out of sight, Mama pulled a bottle of milk out of her jacket pocket. She had not forgotten me. I sucked out every drop.

"Don't tell Papa," she smiled. "He'll just say, 'you're spoilin' that pig rotten'." I love Mama.

The warm milk made me sleepy. The next thing I knew it was morning. I had slept all night.

The rays of the morning sun seemed to turn my straw pile into golden threads. Surprisingly, the straw pile was a mighty fine bed.

Sometime in the night a quiet visitor had crept into my pen. There on the straw, curled in a ball, lay a tuckered out Tom Cat, sound asleep.

Chapter 5.

A CURE FOR LONELINESS

PAPA came by early. As soon as he checked my food and water he made a quick exit. T.C. headed out to find breakfast as soon as his eyes were open. So here I am, just me and myself.

The day dragged on and on ----and on. Hours seemed like days! By the middle of the afternoon I was so lonesome --I felt sick! My head hurt! My belly sounded like buzzing bees! But most of all I felt as if I had been deserted. Where were my friends? Other hogs may get by on food and water only. But me, I need -----companionship. The machine shed was a prison! I was the only prisoner. Everybody else was free to come and go as they pleased, except me!

It was long toward evening when Mama and Mitzi finally showed up. I dug in under the straw pile and refused to come out. Sounds crazy, I suppose. But I felt like hiding from everybody. Confused I guess.

Mama reached into the straw and lifted me out. I refused to look at her. I'd show her, I thought! She flopped down in my pen and loved me up tight in her arms.

"Priscilla, my darling, you haven't eaten a bite. What am I going to do with you? You'll get sick if you don't eat. It's just not natural for a pig to shun food," she cried.

Natural? What's natural? I'm not even sure I'm a pig. But one thing I *was* sure of. I felt ashamed because I had made Mama cry and I knew I was too heavy for her to hold. That's what got me kicked out of the house in the first place.

Wiggling free from her arms I hurried over to my feed box. The pellets did taste better with someone there. I wonder why?

Trying to make me feel better, Mitzi jumped around my pen barking her head off.

"Let's go play in your yard, Priscilla," she begged.

"Be quiet, Mitzi," Mama shouted, "let her eat!"

Having announced that Papa must take a look at me, Mama sped off to find him. My *condition* had really upset her. In her frame of mind she forgot to shut my gate.

Quicker than you can say "spit" I leaped through the open gate. The rear door of the station wagon was open. I jumped right in. Maybe, just maybe, they'd take me back home. Hadn't Mama been sad about my condition? Was it too much to hope for? It would be glorious to be home once again. I lay down in the back seat and cried!

It didn't take them long to find me! When Mama returned with Papa and found my gate open and Mitzi bouncing up and down by the car, it wasn't hard to figure out where I was.

"I can't bear to see her this way," Mama said sadly.

Papa reached in the car and petted my head. "Poor little thing! She's so confused, so unhappy. I hate to take her back inside."

He *can't* take me back to that pig pen, I thought. I moaned and cried and didn't care who saw me. I didn't care about being brave any more. Nobody ever told me about loneliness.

"I can't do this to her, Papa. There has got to be another way. We've taken her from her home. It's not good for her to be alone. She's still a baby. We've expected too much too soon," Mama said. "Let's take turns staying with her for a few days. Mitzi can help us."

Mama's notion sounded awfully good to me. Having company would be the next best thing to going home. I stopped bawling. Mitzi liked the new plan. She volunteered to stay the night.

Papa wasn't too sure about it. "How long can we keep it up?" he asked.

All of a sudden Mama's expression changed. She was getting excited about something, "*I have an idea. It just struck me. I don't know why we didn't think of it sooner.*" Mama was smiling the dandiest smile I had ever seen. Her burst of pleasure was contagious. In fact it was kind of crazy. I started feeling happy and I didn't even know what she was talking about. But I felt something good was in store for me.

"Is it a surprise?" I asked Mama.

"Yes, Priscilla," Mama answered, "and it will come to pass very soon."

"What did she say?" Papa looked funny. It's strange he can't understand me, when Mama can.

"Priscilla wanted to know if it was a surprise," Mama told him. He just shook his head.

It wasn't half bad going back inside knowing Mitzi would be staying the night. Going in, Mama reached in her jacket pocket and pulled out a bottle of milk, right in front of Papa.

"You're spoiling that talkin' pig," Papa grinned.

Papa carried me in. Mama fed me the bottle of milk. Mitzi stayed the night and I was much happier.

Next morning Papa brought food for Mitzi. There was sunshine in his face when he noticed my feed box was empty. I was glad. Sure enough, I had eaten every bite.

For the next few days either Mama or Papa was there during the day. Mitzi stayed the nights. The

Tom Cat came and went. He came when Mitzi went and went when Mitzi came. You know what I mean.

One morning my "parents" arrived bringing all kinds of stuff. They brought lumber, saws, hammers and a bucket of nails. By the end of the day. my pad, as T.C. calls it, was double in size. Now that I'm eating I guess they think I'm going to grow a lot.

During the day the noise of the hammering drove Mitzi and me out to my fenced yard. When Mitzi ran off to play in the orchard, T.C. came down from his perch.

"Hear you're getting a room mate," he said, tossing his head toward the new construction.

"Where have you been? Haven't you noticed that I have a room mate already?" I snapped. I was still aggravated at T.C. for leaving me all alone when I really needed a friend.

"That pooch? She's temporary." He grinned, not seeming to mind my anger. It wasn't my nature to hold a grudge, least of all at a character like this Tom Cat. Before I knew it he had charmed me completely and I was not mad at him anymore.

"What do you know that I don't, Tom Cat?" I asked. I was anxious to hear all about it. "Who will my room mate be? A pig? One my age? Will she like me? Or is it a *he*? And,---"

"Hold it, Pig," T.C. laughed. "If I don't know who it's gonna be, *nobody* knows who it's gonna be.

I'd say, it's the best kept secret on the place. We are all in for a surprise! All I know is this. I overheard your 'Mama' saying it was time to move in a mild mannered hog, now that you are adjusting to your pen."

"Wow! I'm adjusting, I'm adjusting! Did she really say that ---that I'm adjusting? I *want* them to be proud of me." I felt like I was smiling all over. I looked to see if my tail was smiling. I couldn't tell.

"She said it, kid. But ya better hold those giggles. You might not be so happy when another pesky porker invades your privacy."

"I feel too good to be uneasy," I told him. "I'll just wait and see."

Early that same evening things began to happen. There was a commotion in the orchard. T.C. jumped up to the rafters. I shot outside to see what was going on.

I couldn't believe what I saw! There was this big, beautiful sow --walking in front of Mama and Papa! Why did she look familiar to me? She must have been a hundred times my size! Was this my room mate? If this is Mama's surprise, it sure is a big one!

Papa opened my little green gate. *That* sow will never make it through *my* little gate, I thought. But she did. She cleared the gate with room to spare. How *graceful* she is!

I'll bet she could win a beauty contest!

All I could do was stare at her. Finally, I ran inside. I did not know what to say, and even if I did I lacked the courage to say it. She looked so ---elegant! I felt --young and empty headed, but most of all, I was scared.

Mama was watching me. I knew she was concerned. I tripped clumsily over to the corner, stood behind my straw pile, and watched. The sow gave me a pleasant glance.

T.C. called down to me from the tractor seat. "You're lucky, Porker." I wondered what he meant by that. Am I lucky or am I not?

I didn't take my eyes off the new resident. She tried to eat some of my pellets but my feed box was

too small for her mouth. Papa snickered about that.
"Don't worry, Hotsie, I'll bring in your feeder and
some sow pellets," he said. Well! It was quite ap-
parent that Papa favored this sow. He called her
"Hotsie". A feeling burst forth in me that I had never
felt before. I was jealous. And I was reasonably sure
that this was the sow that Papa calls his queen, the
one he shows off to all his friends.

Everybody was bossing me. "Talk to her, Priscilla," Mama said. Papa said the same thing. Even
Mitzi was telling me to be more friendly. The idea! I
didn't feel like being anything, ----except a spectator.
Why are they rushing me?

T.C. sat on his perch looking disgusted, the thing
he does best. But I knew he loved the excitement.

Would Hotsie make fun of me too, like the other
sows did? Could it be that she was in the farrowing
barn that day when they all laughed at me and called
me names? She *probably* was.

Papa brought in a round rubber tub for Hotsie's
water and a big "V" shaped wooden box for her pellets. My, she must eat a lot, I thought. Then Papa
emptied a sack of sow pellets in her feed box. Her
pellets were a lot bigger than mine. No wonder she's
so fat!

Mama came in and gave me a hug. "Give her a
chance, Priscilla," she said, in a kind, quiet voice.
"She won't harm you. It's not her nature. If you like

her, I'll leave her here. If you *don't* like her ---we'll give you a few days to make up your mind and then I'll make sure Papa takes her out."

I wanted to make Mama proud of me but I could not help asking. "Won't I ever get to go home with you again Mama?"

"This is your home now darling," she said. "You are getting older and larger each day. You have already made considerable progress here, but you have lots to learn yet about your own kind. You can learn from Hotsie and *you must learn* before you grow up." Mama hugged me one more time. Then she and Papa left. I was plenty worried.

"You need not be afraid of me, Priscilla," Hotsie said. "I'm here to keep you company and assist you in any way I can. Are you Mabel's daughter? Are you the one who's been living in the house?"

Here it comes. She's pumping up her lungs to blast out at me! To heck with her! I just won't answer her questions!

"Don't be afraid of me," she repeated. "You talk to me when you are ready." She walked out in the yard and lay down on my favorite lying down place. *Some nerve!*

Chapter 6.

LEARNING AND SHARING

TOM CAT dropped in, in somewhat of a huff. In fact, he commenced to throw a real fit. "Priscilla! Is your brain out to lunch? What's the matter with you? You're lucky! You get a rose for a room mate. And what do you do? You treat her like a prickly prune! You've got a problem! You, you are the one who was so all fire worried about other porkers liking you. So, what do you do? You're nasty to the first one you meet, who, by the way, happens to be the finest hog on the place!"

"But nobody told me she was coming!" I said. "They just 'sprung' her on me. All of a sudden *here she was! What was I supposed to do?*"

"Be *friendly*. Your Mama has gone to a lot of trouble for you, Porker. Look at this! A whole new

38

wing added to your pad just so *you* can have some company! And Hotsie, she's a good ol' girl! Everybody likes Hotsie!"

What have I done? The Tom Cat would not lie to me about such an important matter. I had it coming. Bawling me out was letting me off too easy. He probably should have slugged me. I was so ashamed of myself. I hurried out to the yard to try to make amends, but Hotsie was asleep.

"She's asleep," I whispered to T.C.

"She won't sleep forever," he answered.

Maybe not. But it sure seemed like it. I kept on watching the big sow, hoping she took short naps. No chance! She slept and snored and snored and slept some more.

Meantime I got to thinking about what she had asked me, if I was Mabel's baby? I think she already knows.

Watching the sow sleep made me sleepy too. I fluffed up my straw and fell asleep, but as soon as Hotsie begin to stir ---I woke up.

She was noticeably slow about getting up. But then, there's a lot more of her to get off the ground. Her "start ups" take longer than my "get ups".

"Good morning," I said, not knowing what else to say. It was my first try at being polite to a hog and I wasn't about to blow it this time.

Hotsie smiled at me. "Good morning," she

answered.

"It really isn't morning you know. You just took a long nap." Couldn't have her think that I didn't know night from day.

"I'm pleased you are talking to me, Priscilla. Perhaps my questions earlier bothered you. You must think me quite nosey. I didn't mean to pry into your affairs." Hotsie said softly.

"Oh! That's all right," I answered quickly. "I have a lot to learn about myself. You guessed right about me. That old sow, Mabel, she *was* my mother, but *not* anymore." From Hotsie's expression I could see I had shocked her. "Did Mama and Papa put you in here to teach me to act like a pig?" I giggled.

Hotsie didn't answer. She just stared at me with her mouth wide open. The poor sow! I guess she was trying to figure me out.

"Mama and Papa?" she questioned. "Is that what you call the Mr. and Mrs.?" I don't think she was judging me. If she was annoyed I could not detect it. Her questions had the sound of surprise and somewhat like she was trying to solve a riddle. I was the riddle!

"I've *always* called them Mama and Papa. They were my 'parents' while I was growing up, and still are. You gonna yell at me about it?" I asked, feeling sure she would! But then I got the surprise of my life.

"Priscilla! Why should I *yell* at you for something

as lovely as that? We are fortunate to have the Mr. ----
or that is, your Mama and Papa to care for us. We are
fortunate indeed."

Hotsie made me feel *stu---pen---dous.* "Oh, thank
you, Hotsie. Thank you." I said.

"For what, Little One?" she asked.

"For not yelling. For understanding why I call
them Mama and Papa. I *do* love them so." I was so
happy I cried.

I had misjudged Hotsie and I must learn to never
do anything like that again. Hotsie could not have
been one of the old sows in the farrowing barn who
called me names and made fun of me. No sir! Not
her! She's far too fine.

There was a muffled sound of applause above me.
I had forgotten about the Tom Cat. He was sitting in
the tractor seat, peering down. By the silly look on
his face I could tell he hadn't missed a single word.

"See? What did the ol' tabby tell ya, huh? Huh?"
he snickered. "Yeah," he strutted about, "you and
Hotsie ought to hit it off *real* good." When T.C. was
pleased with himself he was down right disgusting.
"Well, ta-ta," he said, "I'll be off. Got a couple of
anxious cuties waiting for me. Don't want to be late
---- or press my luck." Thank goodness, he left.

Everyone was right about Hotsie. No time had
passed, or so it seemed, until I understood why Papa
called her his "queen". I could see why Tom Cat

called her the "nicest hog on the place". She truly is a queen and a splendid one at that.

I didn't know how dumb I was until Hotsie began sharing endless stories about hogs and how they live. She talks about growing up with her brothers and sisters, about life in the feeder barn and farrowing barn.

I think *I'm* dumb because I know so little about hogs. Yet, Hotsie thinks I'm ever so bright. She seems to feast on my past adventures. She loves to hear about television shows and birthday cakes adorned with pretty lighted candles, about the time I got to run in the soft beach sand and watch the sun magically disappear into the ocean.

Each time I tell her a story from my past she says, "To think that a pig could do such a thing! You must remember it always and tell it to your children and your children's children." Actually, Hotsie and I were teaching each other.

Papa once said I wouldn't last ten minutes with a batch of hogs. At that time his words meant very little to me. But now because of Hotsie's teaching, I understand. Pigs fight a lot! When they feed off their mother, they squabble over choice nursing spots. Can't prove it by me! I don't remember ever getting a nursing spot, choice or otherwise.

Older pigs find other things to fight about, such as feed, resting spots and a lot of other silly stuff like that.

If I had been poked right into a pen of pigs, they would have clobbered me. What do I know about fighting? Papa was right in his judgment. Not that I'm a coward. Papa knows I'm not! But so far, I've never had to bite or kick anyone to get the things I need.

I know almost nothing about my brothers and sisters. *Their* mother raised *them*. Hotsie said they were moved to the feeder barn when they were five weeks old. When they grow up they will be pig producers either here or on some other farm.

Hotsie enjoys telling about other farmers who visit here shopping for breeding stock for their farms. She likes the way Papa shows off each sow. He calls them by name and describes in detail the sows' fine qualities.

One thing for sure, Hotsie favors Papa. "He treats me like I'm part of the family too, Little One," she said happily.

"Were you born in the farrowing barn?" I asked.

"No," she answered sadly, "I wasn't that lucky."

My curiousity was aroused. "Where did you come from? How did you get here?"

"Your Mama saw me at an auction," she said cheerfully.

"At an *auction? You* were taken there to be *sold? How* did you *get* there? Who would ever want to sell you?" I couldn't believe my ears!

"Thank you, Priscilla, for caring about me. But

you see, the Deerfields owned me first. They were different from the Mr. and Mrs.! Mr. Deerfield fed us, but not regularly. Many times he threw our feed right down in the mud. While we all competed for a mouthful, it was trampled into the ground and became feed only for the earthworms."

"How awful!" I said, feeling sorry for her.

"I didn't know if I should be glad or not when I heard that the Deerfields were selling us." She continued. "I'd never lived anywhere else. I had no idea there were farms like this one and people who love hogs like your Mama and Papa."

"Did you have your own pen at the Deerfields?" I asked.

"Not hardly! Twenty seven of us shared a big muddy lot. When the weather was bad, we all tried to squeeze into a leaky little shed. Once in a while, if lady luck smiled on me, I'd get to sleep part of the night inside."

"Golly, Hotsie, I'm sure glad Mama went to that auction. Did she bring you home in the pick-up truck?"

"She sure did! I had the truck *all* to myself and slept *all* the way home," she laughed. "Do you know what your Mama said to me when I got on the truck?"

"Something nice, I'll bet." I answered, knowing how Mama talks to hogs.

"She said, directly to me, 'How could anyone sell you? I never could. Underneath all that mud, I can see a beautiful Chester White sow'. No one had ever talked to *me* before! Then she said, 'Lie down in the truck, darling. We'll be home soon'."

"That sound like Mama. She calls me darling too!" I said. "I'm glad you went to that auction, Hotsie!"

"So am I! And I'm glad your Mama was there!"

No wonder Hotsie likes Papa, after the way she was treated before. "That mean old Mr. Deerfield!" I just couldn't help saying it.

"That's all in the past," she said tenderly.

We pushed our straw beds close together.

"Good-night, Little One," she said.

"Good-night, Hotsie," I answered.

Why couldn't Hotsie have been my mother? She would never have lain on me. Suddenly, as I looked at her, I remembered where I had seen her before! I was sure of it! She was the beautiful white sow in my dream, the one who saved my life. Of course!

"Good-night," I whispered. But she was asleep.

Papa must never separate us.

Chapter 7.

HOTSIE MOVES OUT

HOTSIE is due to have her pigs in ten days. So anxious about the new litter, she talks constantly! Endless tales. About past families. Each little fellow is fondly mentioned. She seems to relish the telling.

I've listened most politely to her reminiscing, no matter how many times she repeats the story. I adore her. Each day she grows greater in size and in beauty and surprisingly, more graceful. Oh, to be like her, some day.

I know our time together has almost ended. For ordinarily a sow is hurried off to the farrowing barn a full two weeks before she delivers. But Papa knows his Hotsie is better satisfied here, with me. After all, with so many sets of pigs to her credit already, Papa says she has a "doctorate degree" in pig production.

Hotsie isn't the *only* one who's putting on weight.

46

Time was when Mitzi's five pounds were more pounds than I had. But now ----just a few months later ---she still weighs five pounds, and *I weigh a hundred and seventy-five!* Not even Papa can lift me now! The other day I accidently stepped on Mitzi. Boy! Did she let out a yelp? But she brought it on herself, darting around between my legs, barking, acting silly, showing off how small she is!

"Priscilla! You'd better go on a diet!" she barked.

In spite of the misery I had inflicted on the poor little dog, I had to laugh. Hotsie laughed too. T.C. laughed loudest. From high above us, he snickered one of his nasty snickers. Still, he's overjoyed by anything causing the dog pain.

I *am* heavy. That's a fact. Growing is what I do best. I'm not sure about this growing up business. Hotsie said when I reach one hundred and ninety pounds they will move me to another barn for my breeding. I'll reach that weight in no time! When it comes to eating, I'm such a pig!

This morning, Mama hurried in with a tiny brown radio tucked under her arm. Without so much as a "good-morning" she marched toward a small shelf near my pen, and set it down.

How wonderful! A radio for me! The farm house was always alive with music. Country and western in the mornings, along with the live stock and crop report. We listened to the Boston Pops on Saturday and the Mormon Tabernacle Choir on Sunday. My favorite was banjo pickin'. Made me feel like jumpin' around.

Mama was acting strange. She slipped out the door without a word. Didn't even turn the radio on! What's worse ---she forgot my bottle of milk! Maybe I'm to big to complain about the milk, but I *feel like* complaining.

Mama keeps on sneaking me that bottle of milk.

They play some kind of a game. Because, Papa
knows. One morning he came in with an innocent
smile on his face and a bottle of milk in his pocket.

"Mama has gone to town to get a permanent," he
said joyfully, as he held the bottle over the fence to
me. The milk was just as sweet as always. I drank it
down without shame and thanked him properly for
his kindness. But unlike Mama, he didn't understand
a word I said.

T.C. makes fun of me. He says I should be
ashamed of myself to suck a baby's bottle, at my age.
Ask me if I care. I don't! Not a bit! As long as Papa
and Mama take pleasure in fetching it to me, I will
take appropriate delight in drinking it.

Hotsie was napping in the yard. I was anxious to
tell her about the radio.

Suddenly, it dawned on me why Mama had
brought the radio and why she was avoiding me. I'd
bet my supper that *today*, is the day, Hotsie gets
moved. The thought sickened me. I stood in the
doorway for a while and looked at her lying there,
my friend and teacher. They can't just up and take
her away from here. Can they?

Before long I knew that betting my supper would
have been a safe bet. Already, Papa stood by Hotsie,
coaxing her to get up. I could not hold back the
tears!

"Please, please don't take her," I blubbered.

"I'll never ever see her again!"

"Of course you will, darling," Mama said as she kneeled down and put her arms around my neck. "I'll make sure of it. Hotsie has to go now, Priscilla. You know she does. You wouldn't want her to be unprepared when her children arrive, would you?" Mama said tenderly.

"Let her stay *here* and have her pigs!" I begged. "There's plenty of room," I cried, racing around the outermost edges of the pen. "Just look at all this room!"

Again, Papa called to Hotsie. She inched up and slowly turned toward me. A single tear, trickled down her face.

"I *must* go, Little One. And *you* must be brave. You will be coming down to the big barn, real soon. We'll see each other. Your Mama will see to it." She didn't say "good-bye" and I couldn't either.

The loyal sow followed Papa through the little green gate. A tight squeeze. I watched them cross the orchard. When they were out of sight, I sank to my knees and cried like a baby.

"The end has not come, Priscilla," Mama said, stroking my head. "I know you will miss Hotsie, but you still have the rest of us."

As a matter of course the Tom Cat had been watchman to Hotsie's departure. Mitzi had trailed along behind. Knowing that, the cat dropped in.

"You see! Here is one friend dropping in already," Mama said, trying to make me laugh. Next, she turned on my radio. I was in no mood for music, but I did not want to be troublesome.

Mama stayed for a long time. She brushed me and rubbed me down with oil. T.C. hung around all day. When evening came, Mama returned with Mitzi. Mitzi spent the night.

A week past before I stopped feeling sorry for myself. Then I began to realize how selfish I'd been. I wanted Hotsie to stay and keep me company, forgetting all about the whole new family she must soon care for.

I confided in Mama. Telling her how ashamed I was for being so selfish. Mama understood. She was easy on me. She said everybody is selfish sometime. Knowing that sort of gave me back my self respect.

The Tom Cat became a regular Pony Express for Hotsie and me. First thing every morning he was prompt with a bit of news from her.

One morning I waited and waited for him to come, but he didn't show up! In fact, nobody came! Nobody! By mid-afternoon I had imagined all sorts of things and was about as worried as a body can be.

Darn this pen! If I was free to run loose like that cat I wouldn't have to wait to be visited. I could do some visiting, myself. I had an idea.

I took a hard look at the little green gate. If I

wanted to I could break it down! And, *I wanted to!* That's what I'd do then. I'll rush the gate and go crashing right through!

I started warming up like athletes do, by pacing around my yard. With each turn I picked up speed! I ran faster and faster until I was sure I had reached the right speed for breaking down gates. I gritted my teeth, ducked my head, closed my eyes and yelling "CHARGE" ------------I ran for the gate!

Suddenly, a wild furry ball hit me in the head! Ker-Wham! I was stopped in my tracks! I saw shooting stars and pick up trucks! Then I saw the Tom Cat propped up on his front feet. His eyes looked funny. First they rolled round and round, then up and down. Mercy me! Somewhere between my bright idea and the gate I had charged the Tom Cat!

"Whatza --happen?" the cat sounded drunk.

And I felt ridiculous. I really blew it. Meant to ram the gate! Instead, I rammed the Tom Cat. Disgusting! So was the cat hair ---stuck to my nose.

"First, you think you're people! Now you're acting like a billy goat!" T.C. managed to say. He was up. On shaking legs.

"I ----I'm sorry. I was --well ----I was going to knock down my gate," I admitted. Saying it, sounded really dumb. "I got lonesome and worried," I said, trying to justify my actions.

Still cockeyed, T.C. grinned. "Oh, that's right!

You haven't heard the news! You clobbered me before I got a chance to tell it!"

"News?" I tried to blow the cat hair off my nose. "What news?" It made me sneeze. "I haven't seen a soul!" I said, hoping I had gotten rid of all the furry stuff.

"Your old friend, Hotsie, her little porkers were born. Sixteen wee ones! Took her all night! Wasn't easy, but she came through for your Papa. He's got somethin' new to brag about!"

"Sixteen? Really? Sixteen? Ter--rif--ic!" I jumped up and tried to click my heels, but I couldn't. "No wonder Papa calls her the Queen."

"Well, she's a plum tuckered out queen this morning. Her majesty ain't as young as she used to be," he said.

"Is that where you've all been? With Hotsie?" I asked. "Mama and Papa too?"

"All night and all morning," he answered. "But they will be here in a minute."

"I'm sorry for crashing in to you like that, Tom Cat," I said shyly.

The cat burst out laughing and seemingly recovered, he took off for his perch in the rafters. I'm glad he's laughing about it. Maybe I will be able to laugh about it someday.

Papa dragged in, needing a shave, and carrying a bucket. Mama hadn't looked so tired since I was a baby, when she gave me night feedings. Nevertheless, they both were happy and excited.

"Have you missed us, Priscilla?" Mama asked. *Of course* I missed them, but she didn't wait for an answer. "Sorry we couldn't visit you this morning, but Hotsie needed us. Someday, when you become a mother, we will all be there to help you too. Then you'll understand."

I understand already! Hotsie told me about *those things!*

Mama checked my feed box. I still had plenty. She threw out my stale water and gave me some fresh.

Papa was up to something. He was wearing his "up to something" face. He clutched that bucket like it was worth a lot of money. Then he set it down gently in my pen. I wandered over to take a peek inside. Papa tipped the bucket. Out jumped a squealing pig! It startled me! I bolted backwards! The pig ran straight toward me! I ran the other way, keeping an eye on it! Mitzi thought it was funny. She laughed at me. So did Mama and Papa. I felt foolish. What a dirty trick to play on me!

I whirled around and told the pig to mind its own business. It stopped short, dropped to the floor and hung its little head.

Now, I've really done it! How could I be so thoughtless to hurt its feelings like that? What would

Hotsie think of me? I know this pig belongs to her.

"Don't you like him, Priscilla?" Papa asked, sadly. "I think he likes you."

So, it's a "him" is it? "Him" just sat there and looked at me. He made squawking noises. I tried to explain to everybody that I had never seen a baby pig before and had been taken quite by surprise. I was the victim of a very bad joke.

The pig didn't look a bit like Hotsie but he *was cute*. His coat was a glossy black except for a wide white band around his middle.

He popped up again making more noise than ever. I swear, he sounded like a duck! How could a child of Hotsie be such a nuisance?

A horrible thought occurred to me. What if all baby pigs are like that! Poor Hotsie! Sixteen to care for! Wow! No wonder Papa calls her a queen! And to think, *I'm being groomed for motherhood*.

Papa reached in and picked up the pig. "Time to go back to your mama," he said.

"Thank goodness," I said.

At last, Mama gave me a sympathetic glance. I hoped it meant she was sorry for letting Papa spring that pig on me, so unexpected. I'll find out how sorry she is. I'll ask her for a favor, something *special* to eat. Perhaps grapes! I love grapes! I asked; it worked! She promised she would buy some at the store.

Sixteen? What will I do with babies?

Chapter 8.

AN ARGUMENT

THE nanny goats play an important part in Papa's pig production. And, in Mama's pig "saving" operation too.

It was *goat* milk in that first bottle she gave me and *goat* milk in the last.

Only two nannies live here on the farm. Each gives about five to six quarts of milk a day. The milk is *never* used in the house. Mama rations it out --------- like a precious vitamin elixir. Only the needy ever get a taste.

The very fact that I'm sneaked a bottle of this choice stuff everyday, leads me to believe that I rate high as heck, with Mama. That bottle of milk means as much to me as her evening pan of popcorn means to her.

The nannies are called Patches and Gertie.

Patches is a multi-colored, flop earred nubian. Her

lovely coat demands immediate attention. It looks exactly like a patch work quilt --without the stitches. Her name fits just fine.

Patches is always chewing. Most of the time, part of what she's chewing is spilling out one side of her mouth. Nasty looking!

Gertie is a creamy white saanen. Unlike Patches, she has horns. Well --nearly, anyway. She *should* have a nice white matching pair, or none at all. But Gertie is different! She has one long horn pointing to her rear and one stub that just sits there, being short! Whoever tried to make her hornless, sure flubbed the job. Poor thing. Papa and Mama bought her at an auction. Nobody else wanted her because her horns look so strange. She may have strange looking horns, but her milk is delicious!

One morning, a few days after Hotsie's delivery, I was awakened by a thundering argument! It came from the orchard and got louder every minute! The nannies? Arguing? I could hardly believe it! They always appear to be the best of friends. But here they were, yelling and screaming at each other!

Sounded to me like a clear case of jealousy.

Some of Hotsie's pigs are being fed a slug of that goat milk, a couple of times a day. I don't mean to imply that *her* pigs are weaklings, but with so many mouths to feed, she can use all the help she can get.

Patches claims her milk is far superior to Gertie's.

"Face it, Gertie! You are over the hill! Antiquated! Old! Real old! Your milk is clabbered! A baby pig would choke to death on it."

How could Patches be so cruel? This was a side of her I had never seen. In spite of it all, Gertie held her own.

"Wonderful! You've noticed that I'm older. Then mind your manners, young lady! Show some respect! My full development and contented nature give me the edge. Everyone knows milk is better, much better, when it comes from a contented goat. I am blessed with quietness of mind and peacefulness of spirit, the very thing you lack."

"What difference does it make whose milk is the best?" I asked them.

I should not have asked! Gertie stomped her foot in protest. Patches gave me a "mind you own business" stare.

"Don't bother with them," T.C. told me. "They have this very same argument every time Hotsie has pigs."

"Well, it's news to me. I've never been around before when Hotsie had pigs!" I replied. "What's going on here? I thought the nannies were good friends!"

"Don't worry about it, Porker. This will all blow over in a day or two. It always does! You have to understand; Hotsie is their favorite. Patches wants only her milk to go to Hotsie's pigs because she *really* does believe her milk is the best. Gertie --well, you heard the argument. She thinks her milk is best." T.C. Explained.

"In other words, they want only the best milk for Hotsie's babies?" I asked.

"*Right,*" he answered.

"Tom Cat, I think I just fell in love with two nanny goats!" We both held our stomachs and rolled with laughter.

Chapter 9.

ALL GROWN UP

TODAY is my *big* day! I have finally reached the magic weight of 190 pounds. *That* makes me eligible for the big barn. The one for *adult* hogs, like me.

Mama promised I could see Hotsie and her pigs the moment we arrive at the barn. However, that promise was made several weeks ago. For some reason *I failed to gain weight as quickly as I was supposed to*. Hotsie's pigs have been weaned and moved to the feeder building. Papa couldn't keep them with their mother ----just for me. I will *never* see them. As for Hotsie, Mama assured me that I can see her.

T.C. was unusually quiet. Maybe the old fox is sick! Somehow, I can't picture *him* "unhealthy". I know where he is. He's perched in the rafters, where he always is when something is going to happen that he doesn't want to miss.

"Come on down, Tom Cat. Keep me company. This is my big day, you know. It's graduation day! I'm movin' on up with the grown-up," I said proudly.

The cat did not answer. Maybe he *is* sick!

"Don't you feel well?" I called up to him.

"Certainly I feel well. Did you ever know me to feel otherwise?" he spouted. Giving an example of his vigor, he climed to the highest point above my head. He looked down to make sure I was looking up. Then the show began, and so did the show-off. He leaped, he jumped, he sprang and he fairly flew from rafter to rafter, again and again. The darn fool! It made me dizzy trying to keep an eye on him. Why did I ask if he was sick?

"Please come down from there! I'm leaving this place today!" I said. "Frankly, I'm scared. Come on, T.C. They'll be here any minute to take me away."

For his finale he sprang again to the highest point and bowed himself to me. Then, he dived, a graceful, most elegant dive, landing squarely and softly on the tractor seat.

There was nothing plain or simple about this cat! He had made his point. He was not sick!

"It won't be easy for you, Porker," he said, showing no sign of exhaustion.

"Moving? Are you worried about me?" I asked.

"Matter of fact, I am," he retorted.

"You needn't, Tom Cat. I'm all grown up now."

"That's what you think! Since the day you were born your Mama and Papa have pampered you, given you special treatment, and spoiled you. I've watched 'em. They mean well. But now it's going to be different. Those old sows will show you no mercy," T.C. said quietly.

My mind was all mixed up. The cat made me worry. Maybe I'm not all grown up. But I've learned to live in a pig pen, sleep on straw, eat what pigs eat, and I don't drink from a baby's bottle any more, not after I noticed how much bigger I was than Hotsie's baby pig. I couldn't bear the thought that I might be taking milk from one of Hotsie's babies. Boy! Was Mama surprised the day I turned my nose up to a bottle of warm goat milk and said, "I'm too old for that."

Mitzi tore in, barking. Mama and Papa would not be far behind.

"I get to walk through the orchard with you, Priscilla!" Mitzi said excitedly.

"Who asked you to?" the Tom Cat snickered.

Can you beat that? Tom Cat actually spoke to Mitzi! Wouldn't it be wonderful if they became friends. But, that's too much to hope for.

"That cat spoke to me! Even if it was a rotten remark --he still spoke to me," Mitzi said.

"If you stop chasing Tom Cat, he might be more friendly toward you," I said to Mitzi. Knowing T.C. was listening, I decided a little sugar on my words, couldn't hurt. "He is a remarkable cat and will return kindness with kindness. Just try and see! He is *my friend*. A real good one too; loyal and trustworthy," I said.

Suddenly, Mama and Papa were there. I felt shy and awkward. Mama came in and sat down on my straw bed. Papa shut off the radio. I wish he hadn't. No one said a word. I wish they would. My heart thumped like tennis shoes in a clothes dryer.

"It's time to go," Papa said.

"Just give us a few minutes, Papa," Mama told him.

I figured Mama had something important to tell

me.

By this time the idea of being moved in with strangers had me about half scared to death. I wanted to tell Mama, but I did not want to be troublesome.

"You're a big girl now my Priscilla, but you still have a lot to learn. The sows in the farrowing barn may scare you at first. If they seem crude, vulgar, ungraceful or barbaric, just remember, they were raised by 'good' mothers who taught them how to survive.

"Papa and I will never be very far away. In fact, you will see more or us in the big barn. That's where most of our work is. Now here's the good news! As soon as we get there I'll take you right straight back to Hotsie's pen."

Thinking about seeing Hotsie bolstered my courage. Mama and I followed Papa. So did Mitzi. About half way across the orchard I looked back. T.C. was slithering gingerly through a space in the fence. Mitzi saw him too.

Mitzi stopped for a second and stared at the cat.

Tom Cat kept coming.

I watched, hopefully!

Tom Cat called out to Mitzi, "Truce?"

Mitzi looked to me for an answer. I would not give it. She must decide.

With obvious reluctance she said in a low voice, "Truce."

I suggested that she say it louder.

"Truce!" she repeated, this time more sure of her answer. "I won't chase your friend anymore, Priscilla," Mitzi told me.

She means it! The Tom Cat must have known too. By the time we reached the farrowing barn, my two friends were walking side by side.

As for me, I grew more nervous with each step!

Chapter 10.

A NEW HOME FOR ME

ONCE we reached the barn door my desire to rush right in vanished like a pitcher of lemonade on a hot summer's day. Inside was the unknown. At least it was unknown to me and that was scary.

Remembering what happened the last time I stood in this doorway made me uneasy and suspicious. Just thinking about those hateful old sows gave me a headache. Why were they so cruel to me? I was just a little pig! Was it all because I had had the good fortune to live in the house? Their merciless words pierced my heart that day and made me cry.

Now that I'm older, maybe they won't recognize me. Not much chance of *that* I suppose! No doubt, the word is *out* about my moving *in*.

Nevertheless ----I'm still me. Live in the house I did and that fact I am not ashamed of no matter how

67

much they try to humiliate me.

It was plain to see why the farrowing barn was also referred to as the "big" barn. Once inside, the spaciousness seemed to swallow us up. The machine shed was tall, but this one sprawled ----straight ahead!

There was a wide hallway covered with more of those sweet smelling wood shavings. The hallway divided two rows of pens that connected end to end and appeared to go on forever. In front of each pen was a fresh bale of wheat straw for bedding.

We looked like a parade as we filed into the barn. Papa marched ahead calling out directions to us. Mama and I tramped along behind, paying very little attention to Papa.

Sniffing here and there at everything of interest to them, Mitzi and T.C. dawdled well behind. The truce was still in effect. It was too good to last. Any minute now I expected them to switch back to their true characters and commence firing on each other.

The front pen to our left was empty. On the door ------no, I mean on the gate! I must not even think *people* words and *never* speak them, except to Mama of course, and not even then, if a hog is listening!

On the "gate" of the pen hung a small sign with shiny black letters. Mama pointed to the pen.

"See there, darling," she said. "This is your new pen. See? Your name is on it already. You will only be in this pen --part of the time, and part of the time